KT-433-287

Continued on rear inside covers.

Printed and Published in Great Britain by D. C. THOMSON & CO., LTD.,
185 Fleet Street, London, EC4A 2HS.
© D. C. THOMSON & CO., LTD., 2003.
ISBN 0 85116 821 3
(Certain stories do not appear exactly as originally published.)

FORTY FROM THE '40s

BIFFO THE BEAR	SWANKY LANKY LIZ
KORKY THE CAT	MUSSO
LORD SNOOTY	DOUBTING THOMAS
SCRAPPER	MEDDLESOME MATTY
ROSIE	JIMMY'S MAGIC PATCH
HAPPY HUTTON	HAIR OIL HAL
HAIRPIN HUGGINS	ADDIE
DESPERATE DAN	HERMY
DANNY	MULTY THE MILLIONAIRE
AUNT AGGIE	TIN-CAN TOMMY
KEYHOLE KATE	PANSY POTTER
DING-DONG BELLE	TOM THUMB
MICKEY'S MAGIC BOOK	BABE
THE SLAPDASH CIRCUS	TINKEL
CHARLIE CHUTNEY	BLACK BOB
THE HORSE THAT JACK BUILT	ANDREW GLEN
BIG EGGO	ALFALFA SWITZER
PODGE	SCOTTY BECKETT
BONGO	SPANKY McFARLAND
PONGO	BUCKWHEAT THOMAS

THEN AND NOW

Washday in the 1940s was rather different to modern times — but the hard work with washboard, tub and hand-wringer then gave way to the automatic washing machine that is familiar to us all. This first section tries to compare the commonplace of the 'forties to the standards of today.

Sixty or so years ago, washing machines were quite different to the ones we are familiar with today, but someone still had to sell them. No wonder the poor salesmen ached, if they had to carry the machines from door to door, even with Snooty's gang's . . . er . . . help!

Have a look at the X-ray machine that the doctor is using to examine Dan, then compare it with the modern "cat-scan" machine the artist has put in the same picture-frame. Which one would you rather have examine you?! By the way, operations nowadays are far more delicately performed than the goings-on in the very next picture!!!

Sixty years ago, you couldn't stuff yourself with burgers and fries and other similar 'fast food', like you can nowadays. Back then, in The Dandy's 'Bamboo Town', you had to wait for your food — and the person who served you was a tortoise!

Trust the Dandy to foresee the future! In modern medicine, there are amazing advances in techniques such as plastic surgery and genetics, also using glandular secretions and bone marrow. But, back in the '40s, Desperate Dan didn't bother about medical techniques — he just gulped down a full bottle . . . of monkey glands! And it wasn't explained to him **why** the monkey glands will change his face!

The **MICKEY'S MAGIC BOOK** strip shown here lets the modern reader see how washing was done 60 years ago (except for the giant rabbit!). It's a pity Mickey's magic book didn't contain a picture of a washing machine of the future!

The SLAPDASH CIRCUS

THE FORTIES

Marmaduke

"HI, there, boy!" At the sound of these words, spoken in a high, affected voice, Don of the Circus, who was brushing his pony, Silver Star, turned to see a tall sallow-faced boy standing by the gate of the circus. He was smartly dressed, and wore a monocle in one eye.

"I say, boy, is this the circus?" the stranger asked as Don approached.

"Yes, this is Barnard's Slapdash Circus," answered Don.

"I say, how perfectly jolly! I suppose you're one of the boys who do odd jobs, eh, what?" said the stranger in a very superior tone. "I'd like to have a look round — just a little peep, you know."

With an effort Don stopped himself from laughing, and replied, "I don't suppose anyone will stop you, but don't start opening cages or doing anything silly."

The boy scowled and asked: "Who are you to speak to me like that? D'you know who I am! I'm the Honourable Marmaduke, and my father is Lord Doggylike of Great Muckley-on-the-Wold. Out of my way!" And the stranger pushed past Don.

Don said nothing though he could have told him that he was the boss of the circus. The owner, Mr Duke Barnard, had gone away for a long holiday, and had made Don the manager in his absence. But this was to be kept a dead secret and the only other person who knew was Mr Court, the solicitor. Whenever Don had an order to give he told Mr Court, who wrote out a notice which was pinned up on a large board in the circus.

Half and hour later, when Silver Star had been stabled, Don saw the stranger talking to Joey, the old clown. Joey had been with the circus ever since it started. He and Don were great pals.

"Just a moment, Don," called the clown. "This young gentleman thinks he'd like to join our circus. I've told him we've got a new manager but none of us know who he is. The ringmaster isn't in, or we could ask him."

"I've seen this boy before," said the newcomer, looking at Don with disdain. "He's the odd-job boy, I suppose, eh, what?"

"Who, Don?" exclaimed Joey. "He's a clever rough-rider and tight-rope walker."

Marmaduke looked surprised. "I'm a horse rider, too," he told them. "My pater, Lord Doggylike, owns lots of horses and I've ridden in races. I've always wanted to be in a circus — nice easy job, what! No getting up early. All you've got to do is to get up in time for your performance. Then, after your turn, why you've got nothing more to do. Cushy, I call it."

At this, Joey winked at Don and Don winked at Joey. Both were thinking the same thing, that if this boy thought circus life was one long holiday, he'd wake up!

"I'll tell you what you'd better do," exclaimed Don suddenly. "Write a letter to the new manager, asking him to give you a trial as a rider. We'll give it to Mr Court, the solicitor, and he'll pass it on to the new manager. I reckon if you call tomorrow you'll find a reply on that notice board over there."

"That's right, and if you want any tips, just come to me and I'll put you wise," added Joey. "By the way, is your father Lord Doggylike any relation to Lady Scratchalot?" he asked, his face as sober as a judge.

"No, never heard of her," the boy answered, never guessing Joey was pulling his leg. "I say," he went on, "if one of you will lend me a jolly old pen and a piece of jolly old notepaper, I'll write that letter at once. I reckon I'm going to be a tophole success as a rough-rider."

Don took him to the caravan, where he wrote the letter, and Don promised to give it to Mr Court, who would give it to the new manager. He couldn't help a chuckle as he thought how surprised the newcomer would be if he knew that all the time he had been speaking to the new manager himself!

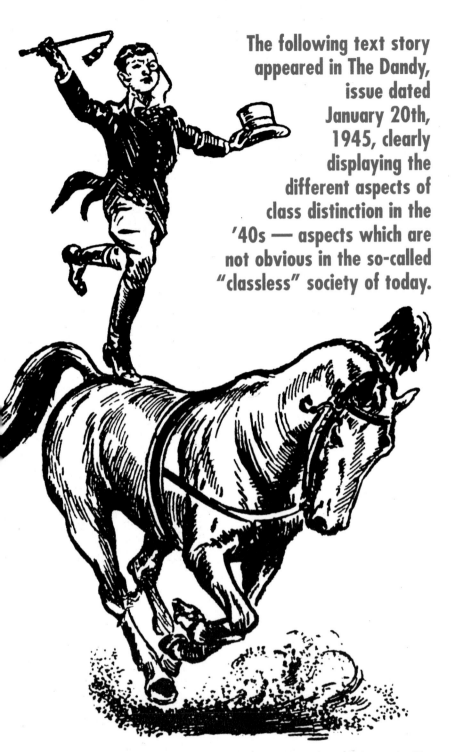

The following text story appeared in The Dandy, issue dated January 20th, 1945, clearly displaying the different aspects of class distinction in the '40s — aspects which are not obvious in the so-called "classless" society of today.

Instruction For The Mug!

MARMADUKE got up early one day at least, for it was hardly nine o'clock when he cycled into the circus and went to look at the notice board.

He adjusted his monocle and read the paper pinned to it. Several of the circus people were reading it, too, while Don and Joey were watching from nearby.

A pleased looked came to the Hon. Marmaduke's sallow face as he read it.

"The new manager thanks the Hon. Marmaduke for his letter and hereby requests him to give an exhibition of his skill and ability as a rider at 3.30 this afternoon. He earnestly hopes the Hon. Marmaduke will obey the rules of the circus as regards trial shows. (Signed) The New Manager."

"I say, that's tophole," he exclaimed. "Now I've got a chance to show what I can do." Then his face grew anxious. "But what are these rules of the circus?"

At this Joey stepped forward. "Don and I will keep you right," he said. "Come over here and we'll have a talk about it."

They walked over to Don, and Joey, pretending to be very serious, said: "Now the main thing is to be dressed properly. Have you got a white top-hat?"

Marmaduke shook his head, and Joey pursed his lips.

"The new manager is very keen about white top-hats," he said. "Isn't that so, Don?"

"Rather! I reckon he wouldn't think much of you if you didn't wear a white top hat," replied Don. "So you'd better buy one."

As they were talking, Don saw out of the corner of his eye, a merry face peep from behind the curtains of a caravan close by. It was Freckles, the madcap of the circus. She was always up to jokes. So Don was not surprised a moment later to see the end of a pea-shooter poking out from the edge of the curtain!

Pong! A pea hit Marmaduke on the back of the neck. "Oooh, what was that!" he exclaimed, turning round. But there was no one to be seen.

Pong! Another pea hit him. "I say, what is it that keeps hitting me?" he asked irritably.

"Can it be one of our careless flies, I wonder," said Don, trying hard not to laugh. "The flies round here are very reckless — they go buzzing about at top speed never looking where they're going!"

Joey almost burst out laughing, but he steadied himself and said: "And now how about pink breeches? We may have some difficulty there, for I'm afraid pink ones are a bit out of fashion lately."

"H'm, that is a problem," mused Don. "Have you got a pair of riding breeches? You have? Good! Bring them along and we'll colour them pink for you. And be sure to bring a tail coat with you."

"Oh, yes, I've got one of those," answered the Hon. Marmaduke. "I wore it at my sister's wedding. Is there anything more?"

"Of course, if you had a blue waistcoat it would help. The new boss likes those," said Joey.

Suddenly the Hon. Marmaduke looked very worried. "Oh, what about a horse?" he exclaimed. "You see, my pater would be frightfully mad if he knew I was going into a circus. He wouldn't let me have one of his horses." He looked first at Joey and then at Don.

"Now don't you worry about that," put in Don. "I'll lend you my pony, Silver Star. She's as quiet as a dumb giraffe."

"That's fearfully decent of you," said the Hon. Marmaduke, smiling at Don for the first time.

"Pleased to help," laughed Don. "Now don't forget — a white top-hat, pink breeches and blue waistcoat if you can manage it. Be here in good time. Oh, and a whip with a red tassel. Gee, I nearly forgot that."

"Righto, I'll try and get them all," said the boy. "Toodle-ooh!"

The Dude's a Dud!

IT was nearly half-past two when Don saw the most comical figure enter the circus grounds. It was the Hon. Marmaduke wearing a black top-hat, a tail coat, white riding breeches, blue waistcoat, and carrying a whip with a red tassel.

"Coo, talk about a guy!" whispered Don to Joey, but he kept his face straight as the boy walked up.

"Oh, what a hunt I've had to get these things," he complained wearily. "I've walked miles and been in hundreds of shops, and now I can't find a white top-hat."

"Come to my caravan and we'll make it white in a jiffy," replied Don cheerfully. A coat of whitewash was splashed on the top hat and the white breeches were dyed pink and quickly dried.

As the time of the trial drew near, the circus performers gathered round the ring. Mr Court was there, at Don's secret request. How they all stared when the comical figure came riding in on Don's pony, his coat tails flying out behind him and the top hat perched on his head.

Right behind came Corporal, the chimp, copying every movement that Marmaduke made. Howls of laughter arose as Corporal circled the ring twice, doing exactly the same balancing act as the dude. He was showing off as hard as he could.

The chimp rode out and left the dude with the ring to himself.

The Hon. Marmaduke didn't know Don had trained Silver Star to obey secret signals.

As the pony passed by, Don gave her one of his secret signals. Instantly the pony stopped dead. The Hon. Marmaduke, taken by surprise, went flying over her head, did a curious kind of somersault in the air, and fell flat into the soft sawdust.

At the same time, Silver Star sank down on her haunches, so that rider and pony sat facing each other, both looking puzzled, as if to say, "Now, how on earth did that happen?"

The onlookers cheered and there were shouts of "Jolly good!" "Tophole fun!" Of course, it was an accident on the Hon. Marmaduke's part and he was surprised at the applause. When he mounted again, the artful pony started to twist from side to side and prance madly like a bucking bronco, tossing its rider about like a sack of shavings. Roars of laughter came from those gathered round the ring at the antics of the Hon. Marmaduke to keep his seat.

Now in the centre of the ring was a large tank of water in which the performing seals had been practising their tricks. After galloping round the

▲▲▲▲▲▲▲▲▲▲▲▲▲▲▲▲▲▲▲▲▲▲▲▲▲▲▲▲

Our Gang are out to win this war, chums—WITH WASTE PAPER! Lend them a hand and send all your waste paper and books to the nearest salvage depot

REMEMBER —
PAPER CAN WIN THE WAR!

▼▼▼▼▼▼▼▼▼▼▼▼▼▼▼▼▼▼▼▼▼▼▼▼▼▼▼▼

ring for several minutes, by which time the Hon. Marmaduke was beginning to look rather sickly, Silver Star began to back towards the tank. Before her rider guessed what the artful pony was about to do, she sank quickly to her haunches and the boy slid off her back and fell with a splash into the tank!

The shouts of laughter that went up was deafening. There came a lot of gurgling and bubbling from the tank and then the Hon. Marmaduke climbed out, soaked to the skin, and his top hat once again squashed down over his face.

"Come along, I'll dry your things," said Joey.

He gripped the boy's arms and took him to his caravan. The circus people scattered, holding their sides sore with laughing.

Don looked towards Mr Court, who had been watching the amusing show, and raised his hand in the thumbs-up sign. The solicitor knew what it meant. He went to Mr Barnard's office and wrote out a notice and pinned it up.

Half an hour later, the Hon. Marmaduke appeared, clad in dry clothes, and Don was waiting for him.

"Just come and cast your peepers on the notice," he said.

Fixing his monocle in his eye, the Hon. Marmaduke read.

"The new manager, having heard of this very funny turn, is please to engage the Hon. Marmaduke as a comic rider in the circus, and he can start his performance in the show tomorrow. (Signed) The New Manager."

Don waited for him to show his delight. Instead, the boy turned with his eyes blazing with anger. "Me, a comic rider!" he shouted. "What impudence! Me, the son of Lord Doggylike, a comic rider! Why I jolly well wouldn't join your circus — not for a hundred pounds a week!"

"But didn't you hear everyone roaring with laughter at your show?" asked Don. "It was a grand comic turn! The Dude Horseman, you could call yourself!"

"Out of my way, you miserable brat! I never want to see your rotten circus again!" almost screamed the Hon. Marmaduke, and fuming with anger, he hurried out of the field.

"Bust me braces, he's in a high and mighty temper," exclaimed Joey, coming up just then. "Well, we can do without his sort in our show. D'you know what he's been asking me — whether we have early morning tea brought to us, who cleans our shoes, and brushes our clothes, and waits on us, and such-like? He's too posh for us! Anyhow, he gave us all a good laugh!"

Don's eyes were shining as he said: "And he's given me a topping idea!"

"Oh, what's that?" asked Joey.

"Why, I'll do a turn as a comic rider. I'll have a white top hat, and a tail coat, and Corporal will copy all my stunts. And I'll do a somersault over Silver Star's head, and make her tip me into a water-tank. Gosh, I'll make the people laugh, I reckon. Whoops!" And in his glee Don flung himself over and did a cart-wheel.

So now, at every performance, there are shrieks of laughter at Don's ridiculous antics as the Dude Horseman.

CORKS! I'M LORD MARMADUKE TOO! WONDER IF HE'S A RELATIVE?

THE HORSE THAT JACK BUILT

THE FORTIES

This story reared its head in the Beano back in 1949. A clockwork horse would have been **very** hi-tech in the Middle Ages setting, and still fairly impressive in the 1940s. The nearest equivalent today might be the bucking bronco (pictured) for training rodeo riders in the U.S.A, which would also probably have been very effective in teaching Baron Grimface a lesson!

Turn the page to read a full episode of Jack's adventures with his horse.

AS BERTRAM BENT OVER THE HORSE'S FOOT, JACK PRESSED A BUTTON. THE LEG EXTENDED AT EXPRESS SPEED, SENDING THE SMITH CRASHING INTO A TREE.

JACK LEAPT INTO THE SADDLE AND PULLED RALPH UP BEHIND HIM. AT FULL SPEED, THE CLOCKWORK HORSE GALLOPED OFF WHILE THE ANGRY SMITH REACHED FOR HIS HEAVY HAMMER.

AT THE SAME TIME JACK WAS MAKING GOOD THE DAMAGE DONE TO THE HORSE BY THE SMITH'S HAMMER, WHILE RALPH KEPT WATCH. SUDDENLY, THE BOY SPOTTED THE BARON'S MEN.

QUICKLY JACK RODE THE HORSE INTO A MARSH.

THE SECRET WAS THAT JACK HAD TOUCHED A CONTROL BUTTON ON THE HORSE, LENGTHENING ITS LEGS. THE HORSE WAS SOON CLEAR OF THE MARSH AND CARRYING JACK AND YOUNG RALPH TO SAFETY.

THROW HIM IN THE NEAREST DUCKPOND!

ORDERED BY THE BARON, THE SOLDIERS CHASED THE BIG BLACKSMITH THROUGH THE STREETS AND GAVE HIM A ROUGH TIME FOR THE TROUBLE HE HAD CAUSED. THE BULLY CLEARED OUT AND WAS NEVER SEEN AGAIN.

This Desperate Dan-sized greenhouse (to give it its proper name, The Eden Project, in Cornwall) was begun in 1998. It was opened to the public in March 2001 and received its millionth visitor just three months later.

Now have a look at this Desperate Dan story from 1942. Probably seen by over a million people back in 1942, Dan had the idea for a garden in a large dome nearly 60 years before The Eden Project came into being!

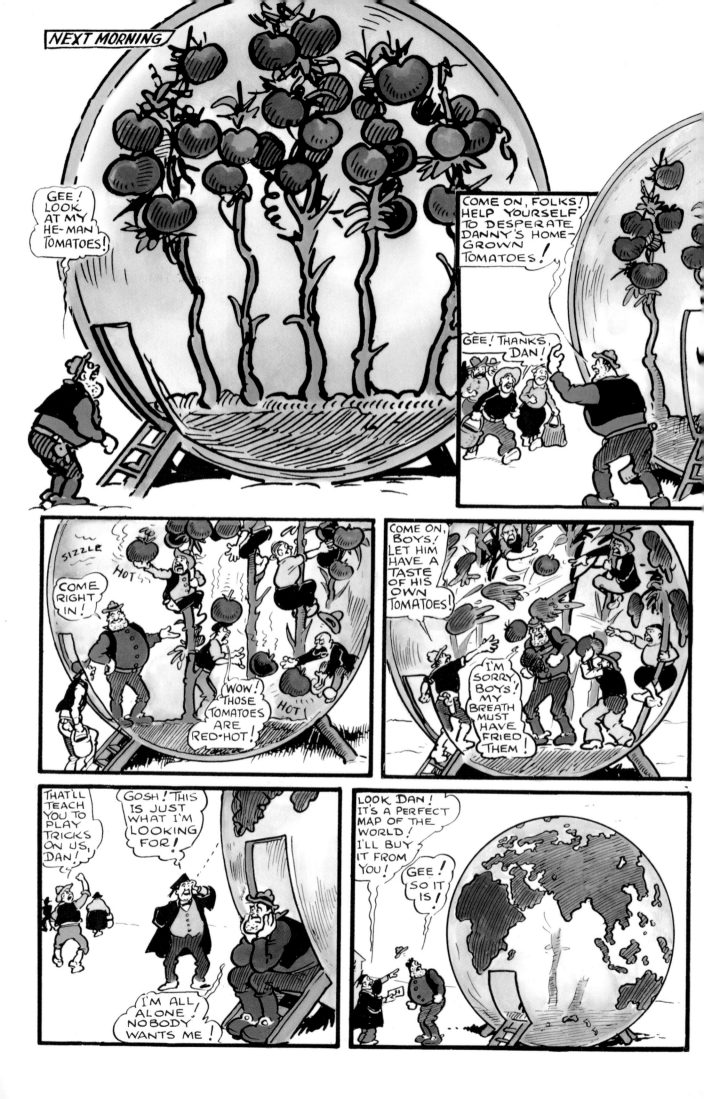

Thanks to the efforts of the well-known (and some not so well-known) Beano and Dandy characters, on the following pages you'll find lots of fun-filled activities which were highly popular in the 1940s, before every household had a television.

In the early days of The Dandy, Korky the Cat rarely spoke. But words weren't needed when Korky battled the mice — just clever schemes. There was always a point to the story, too . . . in this case it was sharp-tipped gramophone needles!

"Our Gang" featured children from M.G.M. short films under the same generic title, with names such as Buckwheat Thomas, Alfalfa Switzer, and Spanky McFarland. Drawn by the renowned comic artist, Dudley Watkins, these cute kids brightened the Dandy pages for nearly ten years, from issue number one in 1937. As they appeared in the heyday of large wooden wireless sets, what would they have made of the tiny personal stereos of today?

The Dan-sized modern stereo speakers (bottom left) contrast sharply with his wireless (radio) in the 1940s. However, the wireless must have been advanced for its day, because it seems to operate very well inside a cave, with no visible power source, long before battery-powered radios were available!

It would perhaps be considered boring in these days of television, video and DVDs, but in Keyhole Kate's early days, a magic lantern slideshow was just the thing to brighten up an evening.

This Biffo story from June 1949 proves that there is no need for either a complicated story-line or lots of speech balloons on a comic page — just a great artist.

The animals of Bamboo Town were 'instrumental' in bringing symphony . . . er . . . some funny pictures to The Dandy!

Here's something you'll never see again — Biffo the Bear minus his trousers!

The radio programmes of the 'forties entertained youngsters very well (even cat youngsters!) but things have moved on since then — we now have Korkyoke . . . sorry, karaoke for the kids themselves to sing along!

MUSSO

The Dandy was first to lampoon foreign political figures, with "Addie and Hermy" in 1939,

but The Beano was soon to follow, introducing "Musso" in 1940, whose laughter-filled reign lasted three years.

OUR GANG

These boys and girls play in the famous Hal Roach films of "Our Gang", and appear here by courtesy of M.G.M.

PETE ALFALFA DARLA PORKY
THE PUP SWITZER SCOTTY HOOD BILLY PATSY LEE SPANKY BUCKWHEAT
BECKET THOMAS MAY McFARLAND THOMAS

1—Down at the fair one day, Our Gang wandered into the boxing booth. The owner, Slammer Sloggs, asked Our Gang to take on the job of sparring partners.

2—Eager to earn some cash, Our Gang climbed into the ring. Slammer's fists shot into action and knocked all the cocky kids right through the ropes.

3—Our Gang hadn't done much, but they figured that they'd earned the money. However, when they asked for it, they were told to clear out.

4—The kids bawled him out till their throats ached. Slammer jumped out of the ring. Our Gang got away in time, but Pete the Pup was not so lucky.

5—Our Gang had enough cash to get into a sideshow full of distorting mirrors. What a freak Buckwheat looked in one, with a head forty times its usual size!

6—That mirror gave Spanky a scheme. As Slammer Sloggs passed, the lad threw a well-aimed bottle, which binged the boxer a nasty one on the brain-box.

7—Then Spanky took to his heels and Slammer came pelting after him raspberry red with rage. Right into the Hall of Mirrors the angry boxer lumbered.

8—Spanky dodged behind a mirror. The boxer's hair stood on end when he found himself in front of a huge mirror from which a terrible monster grimaced. It was only the reflection of Pete the Pup. But that mirror made Pete look horrible enough to give the bullying boxer a bad attack of the jitters.

9—As pale as a sheet, he hurtled out of the place like lightning and in a second he was telling a cop that a monster dog was after him.

10—The policeman blew his whistle to call up more cops. But in the sideshow all they could find was Pete the Pup, looking as if he wouldn't hurt a fly.

11—The cops thought Slammer had been fooling them, so they gave him a lesson that he wouldn't forget. It's a cert that he'll never cheat Our Gang again.

JIMMY
AND HIS
MAGIC PATCH

This JIMMY and his MAGIC PATCH story from 1948 finds Jimmy and his baby cousin Ernie almost starting a war with the inhabitants of Lilliput!

1 — Jimmy Watson was walking along, wheeling his baby cousin Ernie in a pram and reading the adventures of Gulliver in Lilliput. The story was about a sailor shipwrecked on an island inhabited by tiny people — and almost without thinking Jimmy made a wish. "Gee!" he muttered. "I wish I could find this quaint little land of Lilliput." For a moment Jimmy had forgotten the Magic Patch on his trousers!

2 — Crash! Bang! The pram gave a lurch and next minute Ernie was cooing with delight while Jimmy's eyes nearly popped out of their sockets. At his feet were tiny people not much bigger than his thumb. They were running like mad out of tiny houses into which the pram had crashed. Jimmy gulped. The Magic Patch had granted Jimmy's wish and landed him slap-bang in the strange land of little people!

3 — As Jimmy pushed the pram along, doing his best to avoid damaging the little houses, the Lilliputians fled in all directions, squealing in terror, "To arms! To arms and slay the monsters!" Suddenly Jimmy stopped in alarm. Before him was a fort packed with troops and bristling with tiny cannon all aimed at his head. Quickly Jimmy whipped out a white handkerchief.

4 — "Take it easy," gasped Jimmy, frantically waving the hankie on a stick. "I'm your pal." On one of the turrets stood a little man with a crown. He was the King of Lilliput and, now that the "giant" appeared friendly, he came bustling down and Jimmy lifted him up in his hand. "I'm sorry I barged in like this, Your Majesty," said Jimmy humbly. "But I'll fix things."

Now fly further into the book for PATCH 2 of this tale!

Here are some 'comic cuts' from the barmiest barber in The Dandy — HAIR OIL HAL!

ADDIE AND HERMY

For two years during the Second World War, Dandy readers enjoyed a laughter-packed lampoon of the lives of a certain two German wartime leaders, where their craving for power was converted into a craving for food!

5 — The king perched on Jimmy's shoulder, while Jimmy searched in the pram for a box of Ernie's toy bricks. "I'll soon fix you up with a few pre-fabs, Your Highness," chuckled Jimmy, and he got busy right away. Meanwhile young Ernie was having the time of his life playing with two little citizens who had climbed up tiny ladders into the pram.

6 — It didn't take Jimmy minutes to shove up a house with Ernie's bricks, and the Lilliputians who were to occupy it were tickled pink with their Watson pre-fab. But, just as Jimmy was putting the finishing touch to the house, the watchers on the city wall began to ring the alarm bell and the women and children shivered as they heard the shout, "The giant wolf is coming!"

7 — Jimmy sprang to his feet and looked beyond the city wall. Loping towards the city of Lilliput was a fully-grown wolf. It had come down from the hills to the north, and it seemed that nothing could stop it. The Lilliputians scattered in terror, and dived into the shelter of their tiny houses. "Here goes!" gasped Jimmy. He snatched a clockwork car from the pram and dropped a handful of toy soldiers in the back seat.

8 — Quickly Jimmy wound the spring of the car. Then he leaned over the city wall, which didn't come up to his knees, and sent the motor racing towards the approaching wolf. It didn't seem much of a weapon against the brute, but Jimmy had another weapon up his sleeve, or rather, on his back. Swiftly he unbuttoned his elastic braces while the wolf came nearer and nearer, its eyes greedily fixed on the brightly-coloured toy soldiers.

Catch the last 'PATCH' of the story later in the book.

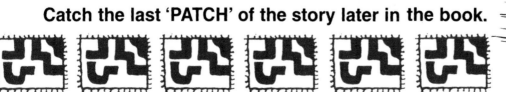

Fashion

THE FORTIES

The following pages give an indication of how people dressed in the '40s. Whatever the decade, clothes will always be important, but no fashion display would be complete without a catwalk — so here's Korky to oblige!

Even in Korky the Cat stories fashions change! Have a look at the outfit the strong man is wearing at the start of the story! Or maybe purple furry coats are back in fashion . . . ?

As a rule, cats don't usually wear clothes, but The Dandy's Korky the Cat regularly broke that rule, and managed to carry off some weird and wonderful outfits, most of which would have been considered quite smart in their day . . . maybe!

Back in the days when politeness was fashionable, Ding-Dong Belle, from the Beano, had her own unique way of dealing with gentlemen with no manners . . .

Doubting Thomas, who graced the pages of The Beano between 1940 and 1942, was to return some years later as a new member of Lord Snooty's gang, in 1950.

Pansy Potter, being a "Strong-Man's Daughter", didn't really bother very much with fashion. Just occasionally, however, readers would see her in slightly-modified clothing, if it suited the story.

MUSSO

*Treacle, fish paste and luminous paint — plus a horse's tail — all help to keep The Beano's 'Musso' **looking** smart, but maybe not **feeling** smart!*

The Dandy's fashionable adventures of a barber had been at the cutting edge of humour and full of razor-edged wit in 1940-41, but nowadays he would perhaps have to be renamed Hair **GEL** Hal!

OUT OF Fashion

The pages in this section are strictly of the "DO NOT ATTEMPT THIS AT HOME" style. What follows are examples of things that were popular and funny in the 1940s, but for various reasons are not looked upon so highly today — that's why they are behind this steel door!

There aren't many people who would walk around town with a burning blow-lamp, but it only takes one Beano character to cause chaos unwittingly . . .

Biffo *the* **Bear**

THIS BLOW-LAMP WON'T WORK. I'LL TAKE IT BACK TO THE PAINTER'S SHOP.

I'LL PHONE THE PAINTER AND TELL HIM ABOUT THE BLOW-LAMP.

DEAR ME! WHAT A TIME!

I CAN'T UNDERSTAND THE WEATHER HERE. ONE MINUTE IT'S COLD ~ NEXT MINUTE IT'S BOILING HOT.

I'LL TAKE A BUS. IT'S QUICKER.

THE FORTIES

BUS STOP

NO SIGN OF THE BUS YET. I'LL BETTER WALK.

AT THE PAINT SHOP

THIS BLOW-LAMP YOU SOLD ME WON'T WORK.

PAINT

This page was "cement" to be funny 60 years ago, but it looks rather horrific. There is concrete evidence that cement mixers can be dangerous, even if your names are Desperate Dan and Danny, so stay away from them!

Here's an everyday story of a live elephant, a clockwork horse and a stuffed head — oh, and two clockwork boys, Tin-Can Tommy and his brother, Babe, from The Beano.

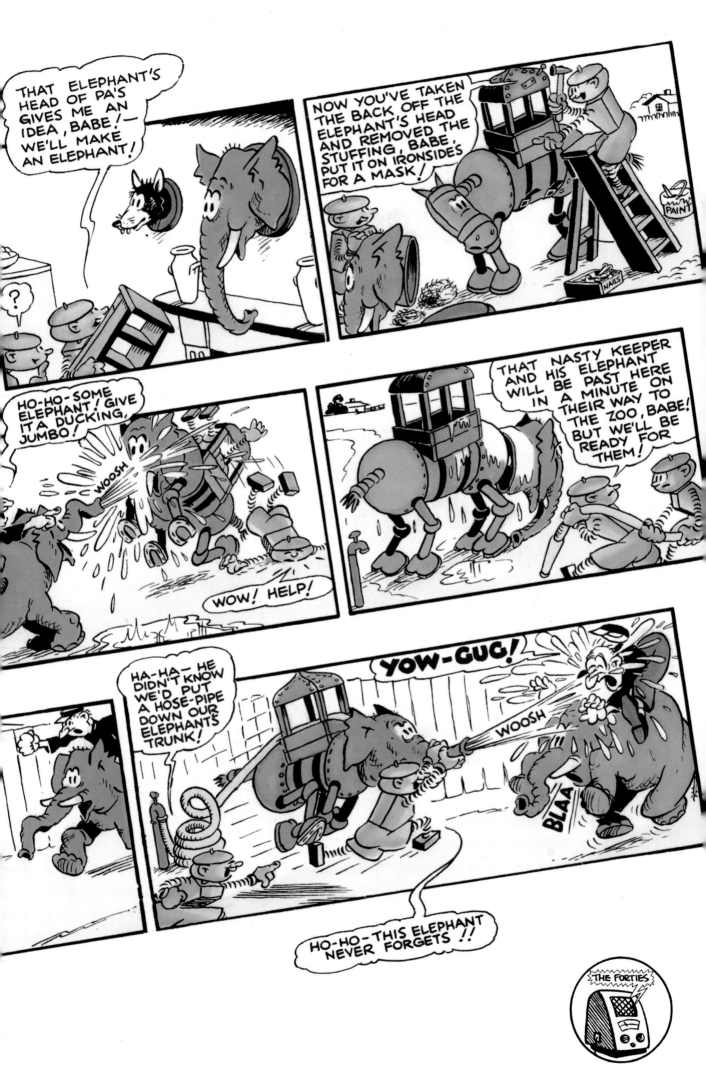

The Dandy also had some "power-full" stories, as this Korky the Cat tale from 1940 "shockingly" illustrates!

Here's another Dandy page that we'd advise you not to carry out at home! But does it make it any better that it's actually an **animal** who is treating other animals badly?

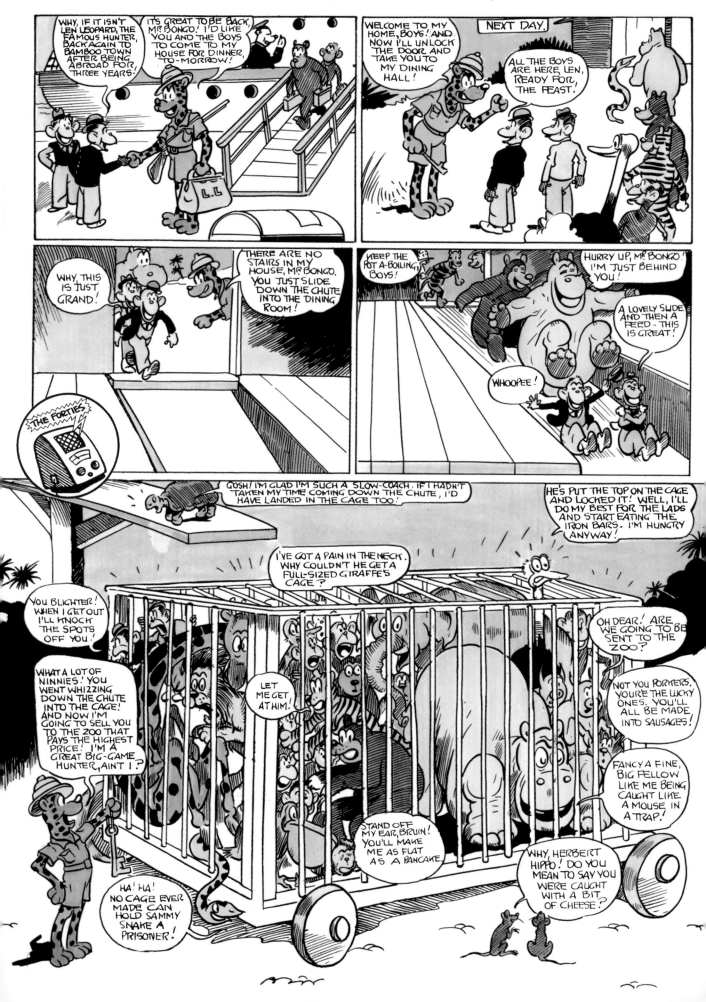

This 1949 Dan page really goes off with a bang!
Readers must not try to copy anything in this
story — just laugh as loud as the fireworks!

More like a horror story than a comic story, this MICKEY'S MAGIC BOOK episode, from The Dandy, might have given children nightmares rather than a laugh! MICKEY'S MAGIC BOOK ran for 177 "chapters" between 1941 and 1948.

TRANSPORT

The 'forties produced a range of vehicles from the ordinary family car such as the Ford Prefect through to John Cobb's Railton Special (which achieved 394 mph in 1947), but the pages of The Beano and The Dandy saw some rather unusual forms of transport, as you will find in the following pages.

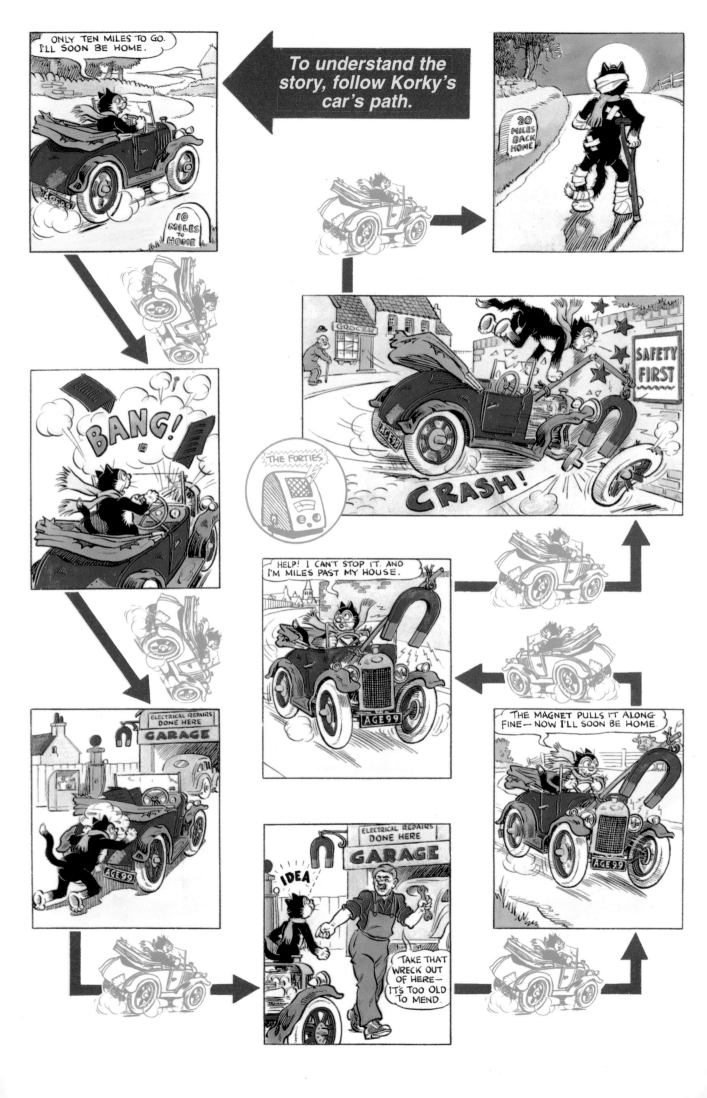

TOM THUMB

An unusual form of transport lands Tom Thumb and his friend Tinkel in all sorts of trouble — until they are helped by some little men who are bigger than they are!

1 — Tom Thumb, as comfy as can be,
Lies in a leaf high on a tree,
He spies a boy, who flies a kite,
Thinks Tom, "I'd like to take a flight."

2 — The boy agrees, and with a grin
He starts to pull the big kite in.
Wee Tom and Tink are both prepared
To fly up high. They're never scared.

3 — The boy has quickly fixed a chair
At each side for the tiny pair.
He tells them both to hold on fast.
They're taking to the air at last.

4 — And pretty soon the string's unwound —
The big kite rises from the ground.
Then up and up the two tots soar —
They've never been so high before.

5 — Then, while they're high up in the sky,
Their big chum gives an anxious cry.
"The string's snapped, lads! Look out! Beware!"
But they're still soaring in the air.

6 — The kite begins to dive and loop,
Then down towards the earth they swoop.
But there's a river far below,
And into it the pair will go!

7 — The rushing water breaks their fall —
And they're good swimmers, though they're small.
Then, as a floating branch goes past,
They jump upon it and hold fast.

8 — It's lucky that they're both so brave,
For see, they're washed into a cave
And over rapids wild and wide,
While everything grows dark inside.

9 — But soon they see the light again.
The water, too, is calmer then.
They're on a lake beneath the ground.
Now see what Tom and Tink have found!

10 — Some little gnomes are fishing there,
They don't expect to catch our pair.
A big surprise that gnome will get
When Tom Thumb sails into his net.

11 — "We're caught, Tink," hear young Tommy cry,
While in amongst the fish they lie.
The gnome has seen and with a shout
He stretches down to pick them out.

12 — The wee gnome holds them up to see
Just what his funny catch can be,
While Tom tries hard to be polite,
Although his knees still knock with fright!

13 — "I've got a catch, boys," cries that gnome.
"Two little men have found our home.
They've both been washed into our caves.
Come here and see the little braves!"

14 — He puts them down upon a rock,
Then all the gnomes begin to talk,
And Tom and Tink bow to the ground
As they are introduced all round.

15 — The gnomes now take the homeward way
With fish that they have caught today.
Young Tom and Tink have got a load —
They heave one fish along the road!

16 — These are the six gnomes Tom has found,
Who live in caves beneath the ground —
There's Nosey, Dosey, Bubbly, Smiley,
Stubbly, and one more called Wily.

17 — Their funny little houses stand
Together, and they all look grand.
The fish are dumped at Nosey's, where
Each little gnome will get his share.

18 — They fetch the dice, and there's no trick —
The highest scorer takes his pick.
Soon they've all played, and by and by
It's Tom Thumb's turn to have a try.

19 — Both Tom and Tinkel make the throw;
But, see, they've had the highest go —
Two sixes! Gosh! Our pair have won!
While all the gnomes shout out — "Well done!"

20 — So Tom Thumb wins the biggest fish.
Soon it will make a tasty dish;
Just see the tears in Bubbly's eyes,
While Nosey hands our pair the prize.

21 — At supper-time the wee boys go
To cook their fish, and they're not slow,
For Tom Thumb wears a hungry look;
It's just as well that he can cook.

22 — The little gnomes are feasting, too —
It seems the usual thing to do.
Though they are just six tiny mites,
They all have great big appetites.

23 — When supper's done, the sleepy gnome
Begins to make Tom Thumb a home,
Though he is tired, he doesn't grouse;
His washtub makes a splendid house.

24 — Soon it is time to say goodnight —
Both Tom and Tinkel will sleep tight.
The pair turn in. Soon there's no sound
Within that tub beneath the ground!

THIS STORY IS FROM THE BEANO, NOVEMBER 1946

Some parts of this Ding-Dong Belle story (from The Beano of the late '40s) were lost or damaged over the years, but the combination of what's left makes a very unusual tale — of Wild West cowboys, a knitting competition, and a mechanical bulldozer!

Podge's VANdalism
with a pot of paint makes sure Bill Smith
has an easy journey through the traffic!

None of the readers at the time would know of
a little 'in-joke' in this story — Eric Roberts
(mentioned in picture one) is
actually the name of the
Podge page artist!

Dan-power features once more in the following three pages, when a "well-trained" Desperate Dan gets the circus scooting along the road again, in this tale from 1945.

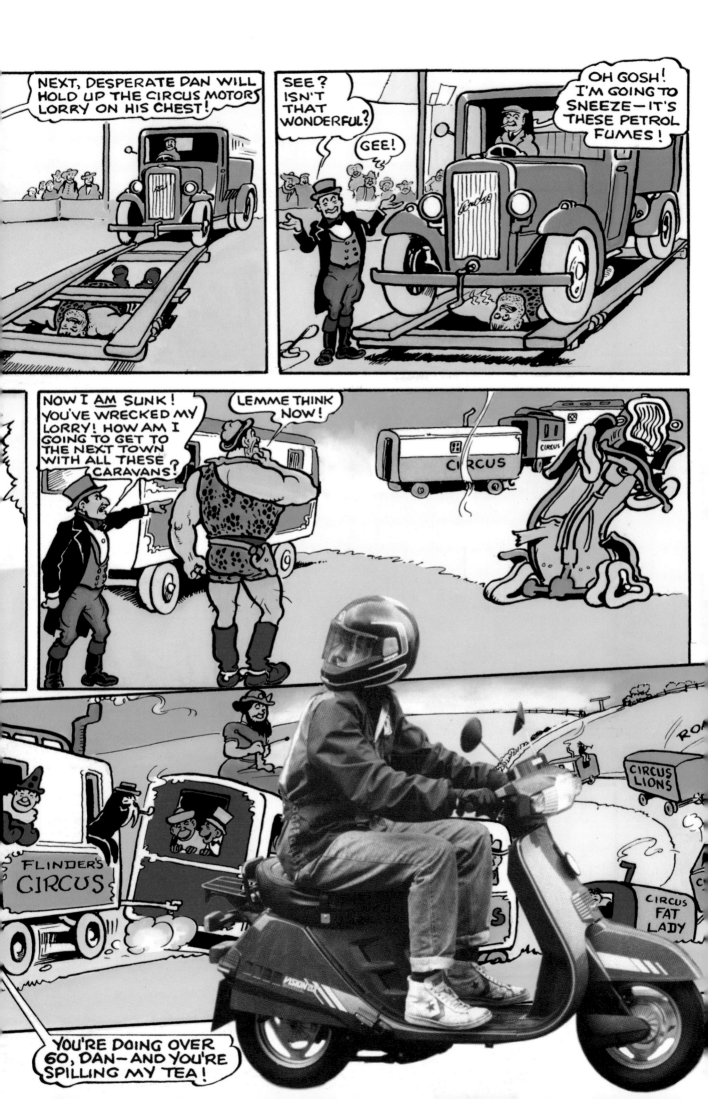

Bob Calls In The Doc.

FIVE minutes had passed since Andrew Glen had disappeared into the distance, and Black Bob was still trying to slip his collar. He was out of breath, and his eyes were bulging, but he kept up his desperate attempt to get free. It was the only way he could get to help his master.

Whenever he paused for a rest he turned his head in the direction taken by the shepherd, hoping against hope that Andrew Glenn might have recovered his memory and be returning for his four-legged friend Bob's hopes were dashed; there was no sign of his master.

Gradually he worked the collar up over his ears. There it stuck, and tug as he did he could not move it any further. It pressed on his ears most painfully. Black Bob began to whine, not because of the pain, but because he knew Andrew Glenn was getting further away every minute.

He lay down flat to get back his breath.

Rising once again, the gallant collie tugged, pulled, and squirmed against the sharp edge of the collar, and at last it came off, causing him to fall backwards into the long grass.

It was a great relief. With a glad bark

he turned and raced down the road in pursuit of the man whom he loved above all others on earth.

Skidding round the corner, he saw the road winding before him, but the familiar figure was not in sight. He put his nose to the ground, and soon took up the scent. At a fast trot, tail streaming behind, he followed that scent untiringly.

There was a village ahead, and Bob felt sure he would find his master there. He was not mistaken. Andrew Glenn was standing in the doorway of a baker's shop, eating a pie and evidently enjoying it. He looked so much like himself that Bob's heart gave a great jump. He thought his master was better again.

Straight across the road he flew, and bounded up to the shepherd, uttering that short, sharp bark which was his greeting.

Andrew Glenn was so startled that he dropped the pie on the pavement. His expression changed; anger shone from his grey eyes.

'You here — again!" he gasped, and took a quick kick at Bob, who quickly dodged out of the way. The poor collie was so shocked and hurt that he did not even whine.

The shepherd returned to the shop for another pie, and ate it inside the door. Bob kept out of sight. It was dawning on him that the mere sight of him irritated his master. If he wished to help Andrew Glenn he had better keep out of the way, and help him secretly. He hid in the doorway and waited.

Presently his master left the shop and continued on his way, glancing in the shop windows, sometimes crossing from one side of the road to the other. He had no idea of time, nor cared where he went. The dog trailing him at a distance grew sadder and sadder. His master was very ill. Even he knew this.

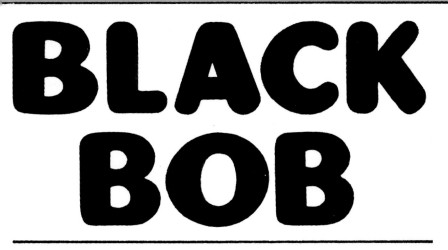

BLACK BOB

The adventures of Black Bob, The Dandy's wonder-dog, were presented in text format long before the more well-known picture story style began in 1956. This particularly well-written episode is from The Dandy issue dated August 18, 1945.

And then, as they neared the edge of the town, a familiar smell came to his nostrils. He remembered the same smell coming from the house in Selkirk where old Mr Corcoran lived, the doctor whom the Glenn's attended when they were sick. It was the smell of iodine and chloroform.

The collie turned and saw a brass plate on the gate. There was a car outside, and a smartly dressed, middle-aged man was coming out with a small black bag in his hand. About him there was a faint odour of disinfectants.

Black Bob's eyes flashed. He knew this was the doctor.

Andrew Glenn's Bodyguard.

BOB jumped out before the man, stopped short, looked up into his face and barked loudly.

The doctor looked down in some surprise.

"Hello, old fellow, what's the matter with you? I haven't seen you before. I don't think I know you. What do you want? Want to come for a ride in the car?"

Whoof-whoof! barked Black Bob, wondering how he could make this human understand.

"Afraid I can't come and play with you," replied the medical man. "I've got too much work to do."

With that he tried to enter his car, but no sooner did he put a foot on the running-board than the collie seized the end of his coat and pulled.

"Hey, hey, you can't do that!:" cried the startled doctor. "What's the matter with you? Shoo-oosh!"

Whoof-whoof! barked the collie, running back a little way, then returning to look up at the speaker.

Again and again he made these little short rushes. Out of the corner of his eye Bob could see Andrew Glenn sitting on a bench at the side of the road, his head in his hands. Maybe it was aching again.

The doctor thought he understood.

"You want me to come with you? Is someone sick?" he demanded.

Whoof-whoof-whoof! replied Black Bob, almost delirious with excitement when he saw that the man had got the idea, and he turned to lead the way.

The medical man raised his eyebrows, glanced at his watch, then hurried after the collie. He had heard of this sort of thing happening, but had never actually seen it before. It would be an interesting experience to talk about.

Every few yards Bob looked round to make sure he was being followed, and uttered a sharp yelp. Straight across the road to the wayside bench he led the way, waited until the doctor caught up with him, then stood up and placed his paws on Andrew Glenn's knees.

The shepherd looked up sharply, but before he could utter a word the doctor had arrived.

"Are you in need of medical attention, sir?" he asked, looking keenly at the other's face. "Did you send your dog for assistance?"

Andrew Glenn knocked the collie away, and rose to his feet.

"Assistance? Medical attention? I don't need any doctor. Why should I?"

The doctor flushed, and looked at the intelligent dog.

"That wretched dog has been getting me into trouble all the morning!" exclaimed the shepherd from Selkirk. "It's nothing to do with me. It just follows me around. If you ask me, I believe it's mad."

He spoke harshly, and the doctor noticed a trace of blood on the side of his head.

"Are you sure you're all right?" he persisted. "I am a qualified medical man. You don't need me?"

"No!" roared Andrew Glenn. "I don't need you or anyone else to mess about with me. Just because some wretched dog makes a fool of you!"

"Very well, I'm sorry!" snapped the doctor, and left, with another puzzled glance at the collie.

Poor Bob felt like giving up. He had thought himself so clever to bring a doctor, and had expected him to cure his master. But nothing had happened, the men had separated, and Andrew Glenn was walking quickly down a lane, muttering wrathfully as he went. Once again Bob crept along far in the rear, hiding himself every time the man turned round to look for him.

They came to the edge of some woods, where there was a grassy bank in the shade. The sun was hot, and Andrew Glenn was tired, for he had walked far that morning. Throwing himself down on his back, he folded his hands behind his head and closed his eyes.

A minute later he was motionless, his chest hardly rising and falling as he breathed. he was sound asleep.

Black Bob crawled forward cautiously, then circled the man who meant everything in the world to him. How he longed to curl up close alongside him, as he used to do, and to put his silky head on Glenn's chest! But he dared not do so now. He contented himself by sitting down a yard away and watching intently.

Time passed, and Andrew Glenn slept on. Once a large wasp hovered uncertainly round one of the sleeper's hands. The dog saw it, feared it was going to sting his master, and made a snap at it with his jaws. The wasp fled, the man turned and grunted; Black Bob got behind him and remained perfectly still until he slept soundly again.

THE FORTIES

So while his master slept the faithful collie kept watch. A little later an inquisitive cow came ambling over, and seemed likely to tread on the sleeper. Black Bob got close to it, and stampeded it by growling.

In all he remained on watch for more than three hours, and at the end of that time Andrew Glenn yawned, opened his eyes, and stretched himself. Bob hid behind a tree.

"Must be past midday, judging by the sun," he heard his master say. "Reckon I'll be on my way."

The mere sound of his voice made Bob wriggle with pleasure, but he did not take the risk of showing himself when the shepherd climbed a gate and took a path through the fields. He kept pace on the other side of a hedge.

It was quite clear Andrew Glenn did not know where he was going. He came to another other gate, which had a notice nailed to it. Even Black Bob knew what the word "Private" meant, but the shepherd climbed the gate and entered the copse. There was a house on the other side, and he seemed to be making for that.

Trespassers!

STILL creeping along at the rear, ready to hide whenever the man looked round, Black Bob was startled by a sudden snarl. Out from between some trees flashed a big bull-dog, and flew straight at the legs of the trespasser.

Fortunately Andrew Glenn jumped aside in time, but the dog came in again, and got him by the slack of his trouser-leg, trying to drag him to the ground. The shepherd had no stick, but beat at it with his fists, telling it to let go. The bull-dog hung on, pulling harder than ever, ignoring the shouts and blows.

It was only a matter of time before he would have pulled the man over, but help was at hand. Black Bob raced to the rescue, and pounced on the bull-dog from behind, catching him by his thick neck.

Startled by this unexpected onslaught, the bull-dog released Andrew Glenn, gave a mighty shrug of his powerful shoulders, and hurled the collie aside. Then he rushed to the attack.

Bob knew very well that he had no chance against a bull-dog, but he was not going to run away and leave his master to its mercy. He faced the charge, deflected the snapping jaws with his shoulder, and seized one of the cropped ears.

But such was the strength of the bull-dog that it drove its head underneath him and knocked him over on his side. He had to let go the short ear, and worked madly with his legs and paws to keep the vicious teeth from his throat and stomach.

The bull-dog got astride him, nipped him cruelly at the back of the neck, and rolled him the other way with its blunt head. Black Bob knew he would be killed if he did not prevent a throat-hold. Leaping to his feet with sudden vigour, he jumped over the shorter animal, whirled around and bit one of its back legs.

The bull-dog growled deeply in its throat, and renewed the attack. Bob dodged round a tree. As long as he drew it away from the shepherd, he did not mind what happened.

Andrew Glenn had not been idle. Startled both by the attack and by the sudden reappearance of the collie, he acted as he always did when there was a dog-fight in progress. He jumped between the dogs to separate them.

Whack! Whack! Whack! With a few short, sharp blows he fended off the bull-dog, which was obviously the attacker. It turned on him, snarling and gnashing its teeth. He hit it on the nose, and it tried to leap at his throat, but Andrew Glenn knew how to handle angry animals. He struck it on the nose again, so hard that it howled.

Then came an interruption in the form of a hard voice from the rear.

"Leave that dog alone, you scoundrel! Bosko, here!"

Trained to obedience, the bull-dog broke away form the tussle and trotted to the feet of a big, well-dressed man who was evidently the owner of the house and grounds.

He slipped a leash through the bull-dog's collar, then turned angrily on the shepherd.

"How dare you strike my dog like that?"

"It came at me. Did you expect me to stand there an' let it bite my legs to bits?" demanded Andrew Glenn, equally angrily.

"It was only doing its duty. These are private grounds, and I allow no trespassers. Why do you think I put a notice on the gate? I suppose you came here poaching with that miserable cur of yours?"

"I'm no poacher, an' he's no dog o' mine," retorted the shepherd from Selkirk. "Be careful what you're saying! I'm a respectable man."

The landowner kept the dog on the leash, but seemed ready to let it loose at a moment's notice.

"We'll soon find out all about you. I happen to be a magistrate. What's your name?"

"I'm — I'm — I'm —" stammered Andrew Glenn, and suddenly went very red. He was just finding out that he could not remember his own name. "What's it got to do with you?"

"You'll soon find out! Are you going to give me that name and address, or have I to put the matter in the hands of the police? I see your dog hasn't a collar. That's another punishable offence."

"I tell ye he's no dog o' mine!" roared the shepherd. "It's been following me all morning. I'm no trespasser. I just didn't notice any warning on the gate. I must have been thinking of something else."

The landowner looked at him keenly, saw the good, honest quality of his clothing, the condition of his boots, his well-trimmed hair and healthy skin. He judged this was no ordinary tramp or poacher.

"Well, in that case I won't prosecute, but get off my land as quickly as you can and take your dog with you. Hurry, or I'll let Bosko loose on the two of you!"

Andrew Glenn opened his mouth to argue that the collie was not his, then changed his mind. He knew he was in the wrong, and that this man could make trouble if he wished.

He snapped his fingers at Bob as he walked towards the gate.

"Come here — you!" he called, gruffly.

Black Bob trotted after him. It was not the way he liked to be called, but it was better than being ignored.

Bosko growled fiercely as they made for the gate, and started to run after Bob.

A sudden command from its master halted the bull-dog in its tracks, and Andrew Glenn climbed back over the gate of the estate on to the public road, with Black Bob still at his heels.

The shepherd shuffled along aimlessly, the collie close beside him now, but still feeling hurt and miserable.

"Where can I go?" Glenn was muttering to himself. "And where did I come from?"

Big Eggo is 'speechless' in this cover story taken from The Beano of January 11, 1947 — is he so tired from struggling to carry the bath that he doesn't have the energy to talk?

This JIMMY AND HIS MAGIC PATCH story, from the very first series back in The Beano of 1944, indicates what life may have been like on a Roman galley two thousand years previously, in 40 B.C. perhaps. It doesn't appear to be Jimmy's favourite time of the '40s, though!

1—Jimmy Watson did not notice the young lad behind him on the grassy bank. He was too busy greasing the rowlocks of his father's rowing boat on the river near his home. The lad behind Jimmy had tied a piece of cord on the plug and was getting ready to pull it out. If he did this poor Jimmy would suddenly find himself up to the knees in water. But Jimmy wasn't thinking about that at the moment; his thoughts were on the old days and the galley slaves.

2—"I wish I had been on a voyage with them," he said to himself. "It must have been fun." At that moment his Magic Patch started to play tricks again and Jimmy's wish was granted. He found himself with the galley slaves all right — chained to an oar alongside them! His Magic Patch had landed the poor lad in a bit of a mess. As he sat rowing between two huge slaves he watched the Roman soldier in charge of them. He held a long whip in his hand.

3—Just then, as the huge man beside him slackened at the oar, the Roman with the whip strode forward. His hand gave a quick twist and the whip snaked through the air and landed with a vicious slash on the big man's back. Jimmy glanced back but was unable to help. The man muttered in his own tongue. It seemed it was the first time he had been whipped. Jimmy shuddered and then started to wonder where the ship was heading for.

4—He was soon to find out, however, for a few minutes later an enemy ship that had been sighted some time ago came within range of the bows and arrows and spears. The Carthaginians on this ship replied with their catapults. These were huge wooden affairs built on the deck of the ship which hurled huge stones at the enemy. That was what they did now. Jimmy, watching one of the stones, tensed as he saw it whizz through the air straight towards him.

5—At least that was what Jimmy thought. Fortunately, however, the huge stone landed with a thud on the metal ring fixing the chain holding him to the floor. The ring broke and the chain dangled loosely to the floor. Jimmy's eyes twinkled as he glanced at it. He had an idea. After a bit of a struggle he managed to get his hand into his pocket and pull out the tin of grease.

6—After he had used it on the row boat he had placed it in his pocket. Now he saw a new use for it. Taking some grease from the tin he smeared it on his wrists and slid off the chains while his two companions watched in wonder. Then he gave them some grease and they did the same. They were free from the chains — but they still had the Romans to deal with.

7—Most of them, however, were too busy with the battle to notice anything wrong. Once freed, Jimmy took a diary from his pocket and by means of a rough sketch told his new friends the second part of his plan. Willingly they did as he asked and, grabbing an end each of the long chain, jumped on to the broad sides of the galley and ran along with the chain dangling between them across the ship.

8—As they ran, the chain caught the Roman soldiers on the ship, knocking them headlong along the deck. Meanwhile Jimmy was at work with the grease and a heavy mallet freeing the slaves. These men were only too willing to lend a hand and heartily set about the soldiers who had treated them so badly. The Romans didn't stand a chance. In a few seconds most of them had been killed. The rest were made prisoners.

9—After the battle the slaves, free men now, cheered Jimmy until they were hoarse. But they had forgotten about the Carthaginian ship bearing down on them. "Get to the oars, men," Jimmy yelled. "We'll ram that ship." The slaves respected Jimmy as their leader and willingly bent to the oars. Straight for the enemy they steered and the bow of their ship crashed home on the enemy craft. The slaves boarded the vessel.

10—The men of Carthage never stood a chance against the slaves seeking vengeance. The fight was completely one-sided. Jimmy, with a bunch of keys slung over his arm, went from man to man unfastening the chains which had held the slaves so securely to the oars for so many weary months. However, after the excitement died down a new terror was realised — the boats were sinking, owing to the ramming of the ship they were on now.

11—Fortunately there was a large island not far away. If the men reached that Jimmy was sure they would be safe. Quickly and without alarm the slaves dived overboard and swam to the island. Jimmy watched them dance for joy when they reached the island as they felt land beneath their feet. Just then he realised he had left the sinking galley — he was now in a sinking rowing boat!

12—The lad who had tied the cord to the plug had pulled it out. Jimmy, suddenly finding himself knee-deep in water, whirled round as he heard laughter behind him. "Think how lucky you are," the lad said to him, "you might have had to swim to safety if the water had been deep." Little did he know that Jimmy might have had to, had it not been for his Magic Patch!

WARTIME 2

In 1942, these 'Dandy' animals countered wireless propaganda with their own radio waves from the shores of Bamboo Town's island! There was lots of **monkeying** around with the radio 'hams' — perhaps more than the enemy could **bear**, but by **ostrich** of your imagination you can perhaps accept what war-time moral this story has **tortoise** — that it's possible for vastly different species to live in harmony together.

Sometimes it's not too easy to put a comic story into a category. This one perhaps belongs in the "Don't Try This At Home!" section, but it fits far better (or maybe Dan himself doesn't!) into the War Effort section.

During war-time, regular artists weren't always
to hand, so several people were called upon

to draw the same character, as can be seen in
these slightly different Pansy Potter pages.

TOMMY THE CLOCKWORK BOY

As a young boy in wartime, Podge, from The Dandy, doesn't quite understand why the war is going on, but manages to get plenty of fun out of it!

Even youngsters could help the War Effort, as
Doubting Thomas accidentally did, in these early

1940s pages drawn by James Crichton (who also drew Korky the Cat and Big Eggo, among others).

Korky the Cat may have been a sergeant in this 1940 tale — but how on earth did he keep his sergeant's stripes on his fur? Also, shouldn't he be on a charge, since he's not wearing his full uniform?

9 — Jimmy was frantically making a catapult. He uprooted one of Lilliput's biggest trees, which was about a foot high, and fixed the stout elastic braces to it. All Jim needed now was ammunition. He snatched a statue from the city square at his feet and and loaded up. He pulled back on the springy braces and waited as the wolf launched itself at the toy soldiers in the car.

10 — Whizz! The statue flew to the mark and hit the wolf between the eyes. With a howl the wolf crashed over on its side and lay still. In a moment the whole army of Lilliput raced out of hiding to finish it off. Bells pealed and people danced for joy. For years the wolf had ravaged Lilliput and now the Boy Giant had rid the land of a terrible danger.

11 — Soon a feast was arranged to celebrate the great victory. Since Jimmy and Ernie were too big to get into the palace, the feast was held in the open. The Lilliputians built a scaffolding around Jimmy and, while he sat on the ground, men streamed up the scaffolding with barrowloads of food. Even Ernie was given a pipe down which came a steady supply of milk.

12 — A palace cook shovelled tiny cakes by the dozen into Jimmy's mouth. And Jimmy was munching his hundredth cake when he felt the Patch tugging at his trousers. Hurriedly he bundled Ernie into his pram — and hey presto! — he was back in modern times again. But Ernie still has a souvenir of the time he spent in Lilliput. It's a tricky little Lilliputian house.